THE BLUE HORSE

THE BLUE HORSE

A NOVELLA

RICK BASS

NL

NARRATIVE LIBRARY

THIS IS A NARRATIVE LIBRARY BOOK
PUBLISHED BY NARRATIVE PRESS

www.narrativemagazine.com

ISBN 978–0–9798727–9–2

First Edition

For Elizabeth, Mary Katherine, and Lowry

THE BLUE HORSE

IT SEEMED that no amount of work or good faith or rededication was going to help them, and they had long traveled past the furthest reaches of brute perseverance. It was up to luck now, and in some ways it was a relief to them both to know that there was nothing they could do. They had traveled even past sadness, as if into a land where nothing grew—not joy, not rage, not despair, not hope—only a dim feeling, some days, like a haunting echo, that they had been foolish somewhere; that at some point, they had missed a turn, had walked right past it, unseeing, and were now lost not only to each other but to themselves.

Robert and Jennifer, who were both painters, had witnessed this misstep in others their age, and older—they were both forty-two—and because a love for each other no longer leapt wild and unbidden from their hearts, it seemed to them that they were being carried relentlessly forward to an undesirable though unnamed destination. They couldn't see a way out. Perhaps there wasn't one.

IN OCTOBER of that year Robert traveled from their home in northern Idaho for his annual pheasant-hunting trip with his friend Jack, who, despite being only two years younger, was a newlywed of sorts. Jack had been married a little over a year and was still wandering about in such a state of wonder and disbelief at his good fortune that almost anyone could see it radiating from him. In the field, he would often talk about his wife, Cecelia, at seemingly inappropriate times: about something she'd said, about her upcoming birthday, about her job. (She was a lawyer; Jack was a journeyman electrician.) He carried about him at all times the unmistakable air of a man who'd been lost or confused—perhaps even unhappy—for most of his life but who had finally traveled out of that wasteland and knew joy at last.

In years past the two men had hunted up in the northern reaches of Montana, in the great grain and wheat fields just below the Alberta border, but this year, Jack, who lived in Mammon, had done some scouting in the summer and had come up with some interesting terrain for hunting deeper into the center of the state, in the country south of Mammon.

The property he had inquired about belonged to a religious co-op. In visiting with the landowners earlier in the summer, Jack had been unclear as to the nature of the co-op's zeal—were they Mennonite? Amish? Mormon? Hutterite? But he was unwilling to inquire directly and was in any case far more interested in evaluating the land for pheasant hunting.

The high plains there were scribed with furrows of wheat and alfalfa, and from rainfall, the plains had steep canyons, creeks, and rivers carved through the soft black soil. The draws and arroyos were too wild for the plow, and there in the brush-choked thickets the pheasants, once exotic to the land but having colonized it with amazing success, took refuge.

The steep slopes drained into low pockets of cattail marshes, too wet for the machines of agriculture, and there too the pheasants flourished, scuttling through the cattails' dense maze, rustling and rattling, clucking, and cackling beneath the autumn-brown rattle of dead stalks. The cock pheasants' iridescent plumages shimmered emerald, cobalt, fire red, magenta, and melon, obscured completely from view.

Whatever the co-op was, Jack soon found out that the people there seemed keenly interested in industry, not so much mechanized industry, but the industry of labor—farming, gardening, and the practice of animal husbandry—and, strange as it seemed to Jack, interested too—vitally, almost fiercely—in the industry of money; though when they finally got down to discussing what it might cost Jack to hunt their vast ownership (twenty-five thousand acres of grain fields, plus all those draws and arroyos, each as Byzantine and sometimes impenetrable as the convolutions of the human brain), the price that the leader, Henry Bone, settled on seemed about fifty years out of date—twenty-five dollars per gun, per day. He might easily have charged ten times that amount. It was as if, in dropping out of the world, they had lost the ability to measure the value of a thing.

There seemed to be no limit to the co-op's labors, however, or to the frenzied, joyous zeal with which they pursued the economy of supply and demand. Jars of honey from their hives sold at the annual county fair in Mammon for two dollars, as did the chokecherry jam and syrup gotten from those brushy draws, each tiny berry picked by the slender hands of women and children, much as the Indians had once picked berries there in the early autumn.

Pumpkins, potatoes, carrots, lettuce, corn, beets, radishes—it was all for sale, all of the best quality, and all startlingly cheap. The sellers might well have discounted their labor entirely and only placed a value on the thing itself—the ear of corn, the lone plum, the single chokecherry, blood bright and held in the palm of a hand.

Before Henry Bone gave Jack permission to hunt, he fairly grilled Jack about his hunting habits. He wanted to assure himself that Jack would be safe and conscientious and something more—something intangible that both men understood but could not name. The whole time they talked Henry Bone's intense pale blue eyes looked clearly into Jack, until Henry Bone saw that there was no deceit in Jack and relaxed and gave permission.

THE EVENING before they were to hunt, Robert met up with Jack in Mammon. In their youth they had sometimes hunted for five or six days straight—hunting for however long their dogs held out—but these days they tired more easily, and for Robert there were increased obligations at home. He was not resentful but grateful for domesticity, and if the marriage failed, he would miss the comfortable, daily routine of preparing meals, keeping the dishes clean, reading to the children before bed, carpooling them to plays, dance classes, ball games . . .

Since he had stopped painting, he loved family life more than anything. Now the scent of oil paints nearly made him gag. He fled from the thought of them, as a woman might seek to banish thoughts of an abusive ex-husband. Occasionally Robert found himself looking at his hands with disbelief that they had once lovingly made paintings. It could have been a hundred years ago.

WHEN THE TWO MEN met at the little high plains motel they grinned, embraced, and eyed the changes in each other, with curious, relieved approval. They were aging, and it was only natural.

Their dogs milled and sniffed, tails raised (Jack ran two golden retrievers; Robert, two German shorthair pointers) in the high wind, trotting about in high prancing show-horse steps, delighted to be out of the trucks after the long drive, feeling the brisk late-autumn north winds, preparing to go out into the fields and do what they were born to do.

"You're not going to believe the hunting," Jack said. "It's like something from fifty years ago. It's like a throwback to the glory days of pheasant hunting. These are wild birds, but they don't run. They just hunker down in the cattails. These birds don't even know about dogs yet. It's going to be the best hunt of your life."

THE NEXT MORNING they were up before daylight. They didn't go to the café for breakfast but drove straight into the country, to the co-op.

In the dawn, gentle hills unscrolled before them, endless fields of cut autumn wheat on the ridges, and hayfield stubble in the lower, moister fields of giant rolled bales of hay, like markers of the land's passive productivity, like pieces assembled in some child's game, with the greatest number of bales indicating the greater worth of one piece of land.

The co-op was down in a bottom, next to a rushing river that came all the way from the snowfields high in the Crazy

Mountains, over a hundred miles distant. The water was clear and cold and fast and wide, curving wildly in braids through the little river bottom, carving out steep bluffs on one side and depositing gentle sand and gravel bars on the other: back and forth, as if in a steady, relentless casting or weaving, or an uncasting and an unweaving.

Robert's first thought as they descended into the compound was one of an almost overwhelming, deep, abiding comfort. Part of it was physical—the sense of ducking down below the scouring high plains wind—and part of it was a sense of the eternal, a relief, on leaving the beautiful but homogenous land of gold stubble above, where there was only one color clear to the horizon, and now in the bottom there was a world of color.

The leaves on the chokecherry bushes were blood crimson, and the giant cottonwoods along the river burned a deep and luminous yellow. Snowberries hung like pearls at the ends of their bushes' branches, and the twisted trunks of the younger cottonwoods were as black as licorice, black as the exposed river bottom soil in the community garden, just turned fallow, outside the schoolyard.

Small children—seven, eight, maybe nine years old—were playing some sort of game in the schoolyard, and though the boys wore somber black trousers and white shirts and seemed already more guarded in their joy, the girls were dressed in long blue-and-white-checked jumpers, with vibrant green long-sleeved shirts, and they laughed and played with greater abandon, their faces radiant in the rising sun. They wore bonnets, and their hair was made up in intricate coils of braid. Some were golden haired, others raven. There was not a one of them, as Robert and Jack drove past, who was not joyous.

Such had been the generations of daily play there across all seasons, that the schoolyard was much trampled, grassless, as if cattle had been kept penned there.

It was a small schoolyard, and in one corner stood the waist-high stump of a once-magnificent cottonwood, its trunk thick with writhing deep crenulations of bark. The tree had been cut only recently—a year ago, at the most (all the other remains of the tree were gone, sawed and split into firewood, Robert imagined, and burned in the little homes of the sect's members, keeping the families of the children warm, as the tree had once shaded those children in spring and summer). But such was the great tree's tenacity that even in felling it the sawyers had not been able to kill it: from its trunk it was sending up sucker-shoots, some of them already two or three feet tall, looking slender as straws, radiating from that massive trunk, reaching skyward, and it occurred to Robert that in sixty or seventy years the great tree might be back to where it had been. And looking at it, it seemed to him that he could almost hear the autumn clattering of those dry leaves, the music and melody of them among the laughing children who would come, also seventy years distant.

They drove carefully on, feeling huge and awkward and alien and not a little impure. Dogs of various sizes and shapes trotted from out of hedges and bright red barns to investigate their slow approach, barking and gathering around their truck. On clotheslines, brilliant blue and green clothes hung and stirred slightly on the morning's breezes. Robert imagined the clothes would smell like the cottonwoods, and faintly of wood smoke.

Both men felt the change in the world, the soothing presence of calmer, quieter spirits, as they drove through the compound, past the little white clapboard houses nestled back among hedges of lilac and cottonwood. The breeze was rattling the tops of the tallest trees, and the gold leaves were falling endlessly, tumbling and drifting—though the tall trees still seemed full of leaves, so too was the ground covered with them, the leaves ankle-deep in places.

That feeling of slower, richer, simpler lives—both men felt it, on entering the compound. It was the same feeling as when one stands in an old forest—a place in the heart becomes stilled. Breathing and pulse slow. Hope flourishes, as does imagination. Both men had encountered hundreds of such places while out hunting, and they felt it here too. It could not be seen, but it was real.

They stopped beside Henry Bone's house and walked through the open picket gate, down the stone sidewalk, and onto the porch. Through the screen door they could hear a woman singing quietly, joyfully, in German, and she stopped singing and came to the door before they could knock. It was Henry Bone's wife, a somber, severe-looking young woman, her shoulder-length black hair uncoiled and hanging free. She was wearing a long blue-and-white-checked dress, and silver wire-rimmed glasses. Her face was pale from wearing the bonnet outside, but her long lean arms were browned. Her eyes were damp and bright, as if she had been crying as she sang.

She smiled when she saw them, invited them inside, asked them to whisper—told them that she was babysitting for a friend, and, as if extraordinarily proud of this fact, took them into the living room to point out two sleeping children, one lying on the couch and the other on the floor, covered with blankets. The children—both girls—were wearing small sleeping smiles, and their hair was tangled though not ratted, as if they had gone to sleep just after having had it washed.

As if Jack had not met her only that one time, and months ago, back in the summer, Henry Bone's wife—Claire—began showing them what she was working on that morning, while the little children slept. (Her own were older, and in school.)

She began showing her labors to the men as if they were already members of the sect, as if they were her neighbors and had come in from the fields briefly between jobs—not as if they were outsiders but had instead lived there on the compound all of their lives, and would be remaining there, forever after.

"I'm at my wit's end," she whispered, pulling a red straw hat from out of a box and placing it on her head. "A lady in Mammon who travels to crafts fairs has hired the women here to weave these hats out of taffeta—she pays us twenty-four dollars a hat and sells them for a hundred dollars, and she supplies the taffeta—but look at this, it's all different colors." Claire took the hat off and held it out to the two men.

It looked like a beautiful red straw hat to Robert—the kind Jennifer would like, and had he been able to buy it in good conscience for twenty-four dollars, he would have liked to—though he could not imagine paying a hundred dollars for it.

"The taffeta is all different colors," Claire explained again, tense now with exasperation, and Robert turned the hat in his hands and saw what she meant: there were at least two other different tones of red, woven through the crown. She had braided them in carefully, gradationally, so that the change was not noticeable unless a viewer knew it was there already or focused on an individual strand, and then another. It was still a beautiful hat, but Robert saw now the difference, and understood her frustration.

Claire sighed, pointed to a huge cardboard box full of snarls of red twine. It seemed as improbable that the beautiful hats could leap from that box as from Medusa's hair. "I don't know what I'll do," she said, though all three of them in fact knew exactly what she would do: sort through all the tangles, separating the taffeta by tone, and weaving the hats the best she could; taking them apart when she was dissatisfied with them, and starting over—tucking the weaker or less vibrant threads underneath, or at the back of the hat, or under the brim.

Both men understood instinctively what a tremendous amount of work must be involved in the unmaking and remaking, if it was enough to upset even this woman, for whom work was but prayer. As if, for once, she had gotten in too deep—had found a task beyond her.

Children began peering in the windows at them: older children, looking like the ones Robert and Jack had seen playing in the schoolyard. These were Claire and Henry Bone's children, and they had left recess and come scurrying over to check out the strangers. Through the clean time-warped windowpanes they studied the two men hungrily, intelligently: not just observing them, Robert realized, but reading them, intently—and weighing their moral balance too, is what it felt like to him. Judging. He wanted badly to be found worthy and smiled at them through the window. They watched him just as carefully, a moment longer, then smiled back.

"Go on," Claire whispered to them. She waved her hands at them. "Go on! Shoo! Back to school!"

The faces vanished, and Claire seemed to relax, growing almost loose in her pleasure at visitors.

"Look at these," she whispered, pointing to some straw wreaths hanging on the wall. "We've been cleaning birds for bird hunters—they drive out here from as far away as Ring-gold and Patchett and Nye, and leave their birds here for us to clean—we charge three dollars a bird for skinned, three dollars for plucked—and we freeze them, and they come back later and pick them up. Victoria, our oldest, keeps the feathers and makes those wreaths. They sell for twenty-five dollars at the crafts fairs."

Jack and Robert stared at the wreaths, impressed by their intricacy and artfulness—it did not seem possible a child could have made them—and praised them, which clearly pleased Claire.

"Henry is out in the fields," she said. "Of course you can go hunt. You can come back later tonight and visit with him. But first come look at this."

She led them outside—such was her energy and her plea-sure to show them her life and her industry that Robert had the feeling she would have liked to have taken them by the hand—and she took them across the tree-lined gravel road and into a large, ancient white barn, which was fitted with a loading dock and concrete floors with drains, and many sinks, and bare overhead lights.

There was an unpleasant odor in the building, though neither of the men would have been able to say exactly what it was. It wasn't fecal or the smell of old blood, but close; and the odor was not improved by the trapped, hot air around them. The men found themselves breathing through gritted teeth at first.

"This is where the women do the butchering and can-ning," Claire said. "We've got heaters in here, so we can keep working right on through winter."

She showed them the hoists used for lifting and spreading the steers, and the home-rigged automatic plucking machine and pointed at the hydraulic hoses, gas lines, and air compressors, the deep freezes, the commercial refrigerators. "Come on," she said, "come down into the basement, and I'll show you our food."

They followed her, anxious now to be out in the field and hunting, but they were intrigued by the intimacy of the tour, and interested too, curious, to see how members of the sect lived. And flattered, as well, slightly, by Claire's attentions—the time she was taking away from her work.

They descended the narrow, warped, hand-poured concrete steps (worn smooth by generations of members hauling heavy boxes of food up and down those steps) and ducked low to keep from bumping their heads, and went down into the storage cellar with her. It was as dark as a closet in there, and she turned on the one dim lightbulb to reveal the bounty all around them: canned foods in clear glass jars, stacked on shelves all the way to the ceiling.

There was barely room for the three of them to fit in the room without touching, so crowded was the space with the result of her and the other members' labors.

It was all neatly arranged and gleamed brilliantly beneath that one yellow lightbulb. The room seemed filled with a golden luminosity.

It was beautiful—the colors of all the different fruits and vegetables, and the lighting looked like that in the paintings of the old masters—though there was still that undefinable odor, so that Robert found himself breathing through his teeth again, even as he admired the beauty and security of such bounty.

Brilliant purple beets, golden corn, creamy young pullets; strawberries, potatoes, emerald-bright pickles, carrots, apples both sun gold and cherry red; and the wine-colored syrups and jellies of the chokecherry; radishes as bright as blood, and smoked beef, and trout caught by the children from the winding stream that ran through the valley bottom.

"We have a full year's supply down here," Claire said, nearly ablush with the satisfaction of her labors. "It took all of us working two weeks this summer—late in August, boy, was it hot—but here it is, a year's worth. We're ready for Y2K," she said, still smiling, and the two men smiled back, not knowing whether or not she was joking. "And the bomb," she said, patting the thick concrete walls, still smiling, and again, they thought she might have been joking, though they weren't sure. There seemed enough food in reserve down there to carry the whole compound through a decade of bombings, and maybe longer: Robert felt nearly mesmerized by the images of the food as well as by Claire's force and energy.

"Well," she said, "if you two are going to go after those birds, you had better do it. I suppose you are anxious to go find them."

They were still standing shoulder to shoulder in the little room: lingering, waiting, it seemed, for the right thing, the one thing, to be said.

But he couldn't think what that thing might be, and Jack said, "Yes, actually, we are—but thank you for the tour."

Claire smiled and turned off the light and led them back up the narrow steps toward the bright panes of light in the butchering room above.

THEY SAID their good-byes and drove up out of the seclusion of the compound, out of the valley, and onto the bright, gold, windy plains above. In Robert's and Jack's lives there was no other tradition as deeply etched as hunting, nor one in which all the senses were felt as sharply.

Each of the men had hunted long enough that it no longer mattered to them as much as it once had whether or not they shot well, or whether or not they found birds. What they loved most was watching their dogs work, and, increasingly, the men loved the landscape they hunted, especially in autumn. They loved not just the shape and beautiful colors and cool temperatures and dense odors of autumn, the geese honking close overhead and the north winds blowing, but also, perhaps most of all, the incredible loneliness that seemed to loom over everything in October, and especially over the high prairie.

They loved each other's company, and the other's quiet sense of self, and they loved the fury, the passion with which their dogs covered the landscape, galloping into the wind with heads held high, devouring the distance.

Jack's dogs, the golden retrievers, were bred to find the birds and flush them into the air to be shot—pushing them back toward the hunters, if possible—while Robert's dogs were pointers, bred to freeze when they ran the bird down, and to point with their nose at the bird's secret hiding spot and to wait for the hunters to approach and kick at the brush or deep grass where the bird, or birds, hunkered as if caged or trapped and believing they would not be discovered.

The retrievers were slightly slower and more cautious than the pointers, though still certainly enthused, as they chased a bird, running it ahead of them, not knowing exactly when the bird would lift up into the air, but watching the pointing dogs work was the most exciting thing for Robert and Jack.

Out on the open prairie where the hunters could observe every nuance, the pointer locked on a bird—the hunters and dog *knowing* that the invisible thing was there for certain, and knowing its location, as they approached, with the tension building—approaching as if preparing to cross through some barrier as mysterious as the one between life and death. This was an anticipation that was unmatched, and in recent years it had occurred to both men as they approached a locked-up pointer, waiting for the bird's final, thunderous flight—waiting and waiting and sometimes having to kick at the clump of grass, to get the invisible bird to launch skyward—that one day their hearts might no longer be able to take such joyous torment, such exuberant revelation, and that on some final flush, the hunter might wilt and crumple when the bright birds leapt into the sky, the order of things finally reversing: the pursuer being undone by the pursued.

The desired thing would fly away, leaving the dead thing behind.

They turned down a dirt road and crossed abandoned railroad tracks, on which sat a length of passenger cars and a dining car. The passenger cars shone dully with the glint of oxidized, wind-riven aluminum. The men drove past and out across the new-mown stubble toward the horizon, as the sun rose higher.

After a while they came to a bluff, parked, got out, and looked down into the scraggly country below. A winding river shone brightly, crowded with an uproar of autumn vegetation—crimson chokecherry, fire-bright cottonwoods, and golden willows—that seemed all the more exuberant for the dearth of it where they stood in plowed furrows.

The men were illuminated, standing at the canyon's rim, and some of the cock pheasants down along the river began crowing and cackling, calling to one another like roosters in a barnyard. The river bottom echoed with the eerie and exhilarating sound.

The men took a pointer with them and climbed down a steep brush-choked draw, and the pheasants grew silent. The men's knees were stiff in the morning cold, and it took them a long time to descend, their boots slipping on the hard-frozen earth. They walked with their guns broken open and unloaded for safety.

Once or twice, walking past the red leaves of the chokecherries (the season's gone-by fruit hanging wizened as raisins), and past the tiny white globes of the snowberries, and then, down on the bottom, into the yellow and green lattice of willows and cottonwoods, Robert felt a tiny echo inside him as some distant part of him tried, as if from memory alone, to respond artistically to the visual stimulus: but it was only an echo, not the thing itself, and he knew it, wasn't fooled or tempted by it, and he walked on, deeper into the brush.

The dog, a little brown one with a stub tail and lean with muscle, dense as iron—looking like no other animal in the world, only sheets and slabs of muscle—began creeping through the jungle, sniffing the ribbons of scent drifting through the leaves and branches.

This part was what Robert liked—the first few hundred yards of the hunt, when the scenting dog is turned into the woods, or into the field, and when the hunter truly enters the hunt. Wild landscapes had always accepted Robert, opening themselves to him and to his emotions, and he traveled slowly at first, wanting to prolong the season's first pheasant hunt. Off to his left, he could feel Jack moving in the same manner.

The dog was wearing an electronic beeper on its collar that would sense when motion had ceased. The collar would emit a high-frequency squall that sounded like the cry of an angry hawk. The sound helped freeze the bird with fear but also let the hunters know where the dog went on point. Otherwise, in cover as thick as the river bottom, the hunters would lose sight of the dog.

The pointer found birds soon enough—the hawk cries of his collar drifted toward the men, and they hurried toward the sound—though the first several birds were drab-colored hens, not vibrant roosters, and the men could not shoot.

There was no rush. The men had learned, in a lifetime of hunting patience. It was better not to have it all over at once. They could shoot only three roosters a day. Better to savor their pleasure.

BY NOON each man had two birds. The hunting had been good, and the dogs had performed well. Each of the four dogs had produced a bird, each a clean kill and retrieve, and no birds had been lost; both men were shooting as well as they ever had shot.

They ate lunch in one of the stubble fields, the mild sun glinting off the shorn wheat as if shining on gold straw or needles—dazzling gold for as far as the men could see, so that they had to shield their eyes against it, and they felt the reflection of it beginning to bronze their skin, as if they were resting on a sand beach beside an ocean.

Their dogs lay panting in the shade of the truck beside them, blissfully unaware that each man could shoot only one more rooster to fill their limits. The men watched the great cumulus clouds shifting their way across the pale blue sky. For a while, Robert napped, until the sound of his own snoring woke him.

"Some hunter," Jack said, and Robert laughed, feeling better than he had in years. He felt more than ever that he was no longer a painter and that there was no longer color in his blood or his imagination and, perhaps, no longer in his soul. What Camus had called paralysis in the face of the dreaded existential realities. Robert laughed again, no longer caring, really—only mildly—and brushed the wheat chaff from his arms. He had thought of Jennifer, and their predicament— their morass—only twice during the morning's hunt and both times had pushed the thoughts away.

"How's your leg holding up?" Robert asked.

"It's okay," Jack said. He'd been favoring it more as the day went on. There was some circulatory problem in his knees, it was genetic—both his father and uncle had had it, and they had at first gradually but then quickly lost the use of their legs in their mid-forties. Jack's father had died of a heart attack when he was forty-six. Jack himself had had pains in his chest and shoulder earlier in the summer. He was lean and fit, but when he'd gone in for a checkup, his cholesterol was 385, and ever since he'd been on a diet of almost nothing but apples, carrots, and dry grain. Three grams of fat a day. He wouldn't be able to eat the pheasants he'd bring home, though Cecelia loved them. She loved to cook them with a glaze made from the chokecherries that would still be in the birds' crops, when they cleaned them: inordinate amounts of chokecherries crammed into the crops, sometimes nearly a full cup, and still completely undigested.

It was one of the things Robert liked about Jack: how old-school he was, never complaining about his leg—never even talking about it much really, unless asked. And not out of any macho toughness, but rather because he was both frightened and curious, and concentrating intensely, dreamily too, on the great wonder all about him, particularly in hunting season.

THAT AFTERNOON they went to a new place, over on the far side of the sect's property—a ten-mile drive to get there—and then each man turned his best dog, his favorite dog, out into the field, pointing the dogs down toward a marshy area filled with sedges and cattails. The ravine down which they traveled was coated with autumn reds and golds and browns, and the low wet area toward which they were traveling was bright green, except for the cattails, which were the dry rattley buff color they became each winter—and once again both men, but particularly Jack, felt a relief and then a growing excitement as they traveled out of the sere wheat country and back down into the world of color.

All day, along the creeks and river bottoms, they had been encountering the wrack, the skeletons, of animals that had either gone down to the river to die or died farther upstream and then gradually washed downstream onto the twists and turns of gravel bars.

Horses, cattle, deer—even the swollen husk of an elk, from down out of the mountains—and while some of the carcasses were fairly recent, from the winter before, with the hide still stretched tight across the frame of their bones, many of them were bleached, and half-buried in the gravel. Young cottonwoods sprouted up through the eye sockets of horse skulls, and willow bushes, as if ascending a trellis, climbed through the gravel-bound spars of cattle's rib cages.

The men walked on past these things, following their dogs. Their game bags were heavy with the birds they had already shot, and the long bronze-and-black tail feathers bristled from beyond their bags, so that from a distance it looked as if the feathers were part of the men: that over the course of the day they were becoming like their quarry.

Nearing the cattail swamp, the dogs began to get birdy and ranged out farther ahead. Jack whistled his dog back in, but Robert's pointer wouldn't heed and loped out farther before going on point.

The men hurried toward the dog.

The bird wouldn't come up out of the tall wet grass. Robert kicked and kicked at the grass, but still the bird wouldn't fly. Finally Robert had to break his gun apart and unload and get down on his hands and knees to part the tall grass, to try to find the bird—to try to get it to flush, so that Jack could shoot, if it wasn't a hen—but when he finally got all the grass and sedges moved aside, he saw that it was not a bird but a porcupine. The dog had been attracted to the animal's strange scent and was fascinated by it, still frozen over it, entranced, and Robert cried, "*No!*" and pulled the dog away.

They hunted on, then, into the wind. The dogs began to find more porcupines—evidently they were lying down in the tall green grass, taking naps in the warmth of the day and trying to avoid the wind—and at each new porcupine, Robert's dog grew more eager, wanting to fool with the strange new animal, and Robert feared it was only a matter of time before the dog bit into one of them.

It threw their hunting off. At one point both dogs were working fresh scent, and when the bird didn't get up at first, the men assumed it was another porcupine. They had unloaded and set their guns down and were wading into the tall grass to pull their dogs off the scent when a rooster leapt cackling into the sky, long tail unfolding, gold eyes flashing and red cockscomb brilliant—the largest, most wonderful pheasant they had ever seen, and then gone.

THEY FINALLY reached the cattails, where, indeed, the pheasants were hiding and where it was too wet, too swampy, for porcupines. The dogs caught the scent immediately and charged into the dry rattling dead stalks, and the men could hear the dry-scampering sound of the pheasants scurrying ahead of the dogs. The men kept their guns at the ready, waiting for the first bird to fly.

Somehow, it had gotten to be late in the day. It was colder now, the north wind felt sharper, and the light was fading. In a near pasture, a herd of horses—seven bays and a strangely colored, deeply muscled, purplish roan—galloped in circles, invigorated by the north wind, black tails floating like banners, hooves drumming the cold ground, thirty-two staggered beats a second; and it was finally this threnody that summoned the pheasants to panicked flight.

And in such numbers! It seemed it was raining pheasants, and most of the birds were brilliant roosters, getting up five and six at a time, crowing and cackling. It was hard to pick out which to shoot; both men, panicked, fired twice and missed, and, fumbling, reloaded, as more pheasants hurtled skyward on rattling wings. The dogs were leaping after them and howling.

The roosters rose, wave after wave, entire curtains of pheasants, and finally Jack dropped one with a clean head shot—orange flame leapt from the barrel of his gun in the dimming blue light, and as the bird crumpled, feathers tore loose from it and drifted southward, mixed in with the scattered fluff of exploded cattails, a marker for that bird's falling, and a sentence being written on the breeze—the feathers and seed fluff kept drifting—and then Robert hit one on his third shot. The bird cartwheeled back into the cattails, and Robert had the bad feeling that the bird was only injured, and not mortally.

Jack's dog brought his bird back to him, but when Robert's dog ran over to where Robert's bird fell, the bird was gone; it had taken off running, probably with only a broken wing.

The dog set out after it while the men stomped around where the bird fell, hoping it was still there.

After thirty minutes of searching and finding nothing, Robert whistled for his dog, and the dog returned, muddy and carrying the wounded pheasant in its mouth.

So gentle was the dog's mouth that the pheasant was still alive. Robert took the bird, wrung its neck quickly, unhappy that he had not made a clean kill, and proud of his dog's talent to have trailed and caught the bird.

The men walked back to the truck in satisfied silence. Jack was thinking of his wife, idly counting the hours until he would see her again. Robert was aware only of the bright stars appearing in the cold dusk and of the warm weight of the birds in his bag.

At one point Robert stopped and picked up a couple of pretty stones, smooth-worn river rocks to take back to his children, and a clump of sage for Jennifer, to hang in the kitchen. Despair rose in him, and he pushed it away, angry at how it dwelled in him. He pushed on ahead, forgetting for a moment that Jack, with his ailing legs, could not climb the hills as well.

THEY STOPPED to visit briefly with Henry Bone and to drop off the money for the day's hunting. The compound was so small and secluded that it was completely invisible from the main road. Jack and Robert tromped up onto the porch with their birds and muddy boots and lightly tapped at the door. Through the glass pane in the door, Robert and Jack saw Bone give a pained, ferocious scowl but then compose himself as he came to the door to greet them. They stepped inside, apologizing for the hour, and were relieved by his smile.

"Come in, hunters," Bone said and gestured toward his table. He pulled out a couple of chairs for them. On the table were two pies Claire had baked that day, and Bone got a knife and two forks from a drawer, and two plates, and handed them to Jack and Robert, so they could cut as large a portion as they wanted. Jack couldn't eat any, because of his heart, and Robert cut a modest sliver and ate, exclaiming the pie was delicious.

Then Claire came up the basement steps, paint bucket and broad brush still in hand, and in a smock and apron. There was blue paint on her smock, her hands, and face. She smiled at the men, and the corners of Bone's mouth turned down when he saw her smiling.

Children began filtering into the kitchen from other parts of the house. Some of the younger ones stood behind Henry Bone, while the older ones, all girls, stood on either side of

Claire. They held themselves much as she did. The boys stood behind their father, and all the children stared at the visitors as if they'd landed in the kitchen by parachute.

The children kept glancing at the pies, and Bone nodded and said, "All right," and each child got a small plate and fork and cut his or her own portion; and in a minute, both pies were gone. The children carried their plates back to their previous positions—the boys standing behind Bone, and the girls flanking Claire—and all five children ate their pie standing up, like field hands.

Only the men—Jack, Robert, and Bone—sat at the little table. The children watched for the visitors to do something spectacular, as the visitors sat talking with Bone and sipping that bright chokecherry wine he'd offered. Outside, the night wind stirred the dry leaves on the cottonwoods. Robert sipped the bright wine and all felt time slowing.

Claire disappeared from the room while Bone talked on about the falling commodities prices, and the responsibilities of the compound. Their ancestors had been run out of Germany—had emigrated to Russia, where Catherine the Great had allowed them to practice their religion for as long as she lived. After her death, they had been scattered to the winds—fleeing to Czechoslovakia, Turkey, Romania, and finally, eastern Montana.

In the compound there were only about forty-five of them—brothers and sisters, aunts and uncles, grandmothers. There were other sects scattered across the state, tucked here and there in draws, in the canyons on the eastern side of the state, and the members of the various sects were able to intermarry, with the woman moving to the man's sect—but by and large, each compound remained isolated, self-sufficient, and somewhat suspicious of other sects: untrusting of those who should have been, by blood and spirit, their natural allies.

Claire returned with a small plastic sandwich bag filled with what looked like dirt and stones. She seemed joyful. Robert thought she was mildly exhilarated at having visitors. She reached into the bag of dirt and pulled out a small worn object, pearl colored and about half the size of a man's thumb, and handed it to Robert with the pleasure of a school-girl at show-and-tell. "What do you think it is?" she asked.

It was clearly the worn molar of a large grazing animal—the four dendritic splays, the anchors by which the nerves attached to the gums easily identifiable. The grinding surface was slickened with use—how many millions of blades of prairie grass had it cropped? Robert thought the tooth was likely to be that of a cow or horse, but he wondered if it was a trick question—a test. All he said was, "A tooth," and Claire nodded, as if glad he had gotten that part right, and said, "A *buffalo* tooth."

Robert gasped with pleasure and examined the tooth anew.

"Each of the children has one," Claire said, taking more teeth from the bag. "One of our members found them when he was digging up dirt with his backhoe for our gardens. That canyon where you hunted today? It's a jump. It's where the Indi-ans used to drive the buffalo over the edge. The buffalo would die from the fall, or break their legs, and the Indians would go down there and slaughter them.

"They'd been doing it forever," she said, "right up until the end—until the buffalo and the Indians were no more. Our friend with the backhoe said the ground is saturated with bones, and that the deeper you dig, the more you find. Some of the bones are blackened from fires. The Indians must have

camped there and cooked the bones for, what is it called?"—
Claire searched her mind for a moment, knowing the German
word but not the English—"the *marrow*, you know? Isn't that
amazing?"

She pulled another fragment from the bag, a shard of fire-
blackened bone, and handed it to Robert, who marveled at it
appropriately, as did Jack.

Henry Bone gave a pained smile. How many times had he
heard the history lesson? Every time a stranger came into the
kitchen? Though when did visitors from the outside world
come? Robert noticed that the muscles on the left side of
Bone's face were twitching, jumping like a horse's withers as it
attempts to dislodge a fly.

Claire handed the tooth to her oldest daughter and hurried
back down the steps. They waited on her. Bone fidgeted, and
Robert glanced at the clock on the wall, then at his watch, and
noticed, with a start, that the wall clock was an hour slow—as
if it had not moved since they came in—and Bone, noticing
Robert's confusion, said, "It's regular time—we never switch
over to that new time."

They heard Claire come running back up the steps, and
this time she had an envelope full of photos. She knelt next to
Robert and spread the photos on the table—Polaroids all. At
the other end of the table, Bone seemed ready to snarl.

The photos were grainy pictures of a white object pro-
truding from a cliff wall above a river. Robert bent over the
photos and saw that the object was a buffalo skull.

"The whole body's in there," Claire said. "How old do you
think it must be? How long do you think it's been buried?"

Robert could only shake his head. "A long time," he said,
and Claire nodded; it was answer enough.

"It's a bend in the river," she said. "A place where the river cut away some of the dirt. But still, the buffalo is about ten feet above where the river is today. How do you think that happened?" Robert could feel Bone's anger rising. *Listen, folks,* Robert wanted to say, *I've got my own problems. I just came out for a hunt.* He had the feeling that if he showed any more interest in the photos, Claire would offer to take him down to the river the next day and show him the skull.

"Our neighbor's got it standing up in his yard now," she said. "Some museum from New York wanted to come and take it, but he wouldn't let them. Said it was his. He dug the whole thing out and brought it home with him," she said. "Now there's just a big hole in the cliff, where he dug."

"It would have been interesting if he'd left it where it was," Robert said.

"Why?" Claire asked.

"Just to see how long it would take to work itself out, under the natural process of things." Robert wondered how many buffalo lay trapped in the floodplain: a nation of buffalo skeletons, a vast herd still in motion, marching beneath the ground. Migrating.

Claire was looking at him as if she had misjudged him. "It might never have gotten out," she said. "Or it might have taken years." She looked betrayed, and Bone snorted a small laugh.

Claire took the clearest photo from the table and held it up. "He was careful, digging it out," she said. "He had to climb up there and use a shovel. He didn't lose too many of the bones."

Robert admired the remaining photos. "It's amazing, isn't it," he said, "to think that all that dirt piled up on top of that skeleton has eroded from the tops of those mountains. So much dirt—the entire tops of the mountains being worn down."

But again, there was an uneasiness in the room. Claire took up the rest of the photos and put them back in the envelope.

"Did you see any snakes today?" Bone asked. "Warm as it got, you might have seen one. Were any out?"

Jack and Robert looked at each other, thinking of their dogs.

"No snakes?" Bone asked, and for the first time he looked truly pleased. He turned to Claire. "Guess we got 'em all," he said. "First weekend in September we have a rattlesnake roundup. They're usually starting to den up by then. You find a den of 'em, you can kill hundreds. Every year we think we got 'em all, but the next year, we'll find a hundred, two hundred more. They just keep on propagating, like everything else."

Robert glanced again at the clock on the wall. "We don't want to keep you folks." But he knew that in sharing the pie and wine, as well as in leaving the birds to be plucked, he and Jack had committed to a certain necessary leisureliness.

"What about coyotes?" Bone asked. "See any of them?"

Jack shook his head. "How do you control those?" he asked—worrying that there might be traps, or poison baits set out in the fields.

"I shoot 'em," Bone said. "Government trapper 'round here takes me up in his plane, lets me do the shooting, once a month."

Jack nodded. "Must be hard, to shoot them out of a plane," he said.

Bone shrugged, a brush of modesty, "Nah," he said. "It's about like shooting them from the back of the truck."

Hunting all day, Robert had felt himself filling again with the sparks of life—and with wonder. Now the tonic of the day was being taken from him. His mind filled with images of the wild bouncing truck ride as shooters pursued coyotes across hills and plains; the mad swoops of a roaring helicopter; the clubbing of sluggish, brilliant gold-and-black rattlesnakes; and buffalo hurtling over the cliffs, entire herds falling hundreds of feet to a stony death.

Bone seemed at peace: *no coyotes, either.* What did it take day after day, generation after generation, to carve out such control of the land?

The children went to their rooms and returned with cardboard boxes of treasures gleaned from the fields— arrowheads, tomahawk blades, spear points, and fossils too: bryozoans, arthropods, trilobites, and the leaves of intricate ferns pressed in coal.

The oldest daughter handed one of the stones to Robert. "Look," she said, "it's a little jellyfish." Robert held it in both hands, trying to gauge not its history, but hers.

Claire interrupted his thoughts. "It's from the time of the Flood, right?" she asked. The children stared at him, waiting for an answer. The fossil wasn't a miracle but just a common fossil.

Bone rose brusquely and said, "Fellas, we've got to get to bed. You boys leave your birds here, Claire will have them cleaned, you come back by for them tomorrow."

They said their good-byes and thank-yous and stepped out into the cool and windy night. "Good Christ, she was desperate," Jack said quietly as they walked to the truck. "What do you want to bet she's watching us out the window?"

"I don't want to think about it," Robert said.

"I'll bet there are nights she'd come with us," Jack said. "She'd just walk right out the door and not look back—not at her husband, her kids, not anything."

The men reached the truck. The dogs whined and thumped in their kennels and then settled back in, groaning with the pleasure of the day's exhaustions.

"She wouldn't leave her religion," Robert said. "Whatever it is, that's her ticket out of here. Her ticket to heaven."

Jack leaned over the steering wheel and turned the key. "And us," he said, looking up at the bright stars, "we're just going to have to shoot our way out of here."

Robert smiled, but it wasn't an easy smile. Jack had Cecelia to serve, and Claire, her family and her God. Robert had run out of anything to serve, to be consumed by.

They rode with the windows down to feel the autumn air rushing in. Robert held his arm out the window, twisted and flexed it against the wind.

Sheets and waves of yellow cottonwood leaves tumbled toward them. Some swirled in through the windows and landed in their laps. Robert thought of how the feathers of a bird that had been shot would hang in the air, drifting, after the bird had gone down.

There was no traffic. They flew down the road and let the dark landscape fill them.

BY THE TIME they got back to Mammon, there was only one restaurant open, and they didn't have time to shower and change. Instead, they went straight in, still wearing their hunting clothes, dirty from the field. They ordered, then washed up in the restroom—a little alarmed by the mirror's savage representations.

They went back to their table to wait for their meal. When the waitress brought it to them—a churlish silence emanating from the kitchen, and the waitress none too happy either with the lateness of the hour—both men had fallen asleep with their heads in their folded arms on the table.

THE NEXT DAY they were up early, showered, and off before dawn—traveling through the darkness. A little later, as they loaded their guns and readied the dogs for being turned out, Jack said, "This is going to be a good one. Be ready to remember this one."

The first few birds that the men got up were hens, small and drab and brown, but rising with such explosiveness, and at such close range, that the men's hard-pumping hearts clenched every time, and when they finally found a rooster, they were startled by both the size and color of it, and both men missed, shooting behind the bird.

Flakes of hoarfrost fell from the bird's wings as it made its escape, flying directly into the sun; and after the bird was gone, they could still see the shining column of ice crystals glittering in the sunlight.

At the sound of the gunfire, the remaining birds moved out ahead of them, running, and the dogs ran to stay with them. The men hurried along behind. Robert's pointer pinned a big rooster, and Jack sent his retriever in to flush it. Robert made the shot as the bird flew low and fast across a beaver slough, so that the retriever had to swim across the creek to fetch it. The dog leapt into the cold water with an exuberance that made the men laugh out loud.

There were birds getting up all around them. In the rich excess of the morning, it seemed a shame that they could take only three birds. Soon they had a pair each and had to simply watch as the birds flew away. They each saved one bird on their limit, not wanting the hunt to end too soon. It was their last day. Jack was anxious to see Cecelia, and Robert would be glad to see Jennifer, as he always was glad to see her after any absence. *Twenty years*. He pushed the thought away.

To prolong the hunt, the men turned toward the plains and followed the fence lines. Robert had read that ranchers were experimenting with using strands of polyethylene barbed wire and plastic fence posts, and he hoped that such a thing would not come to pass in his lifetime. He turned to mention it to Jack and was surprised to see that Jack had fallen behind and was favoring his leg more than usual. Robert stopped and waited.

Jack reached him, breathing hard, and they rested a while. The panting dogs returned to them, whirling around their feet, eyes bright and mouths grinning. The men watered the dogs, and Jack said, "I guess we'd better go get that third bird."

A half a mile away, there was another canyon. It was a broad valley lush with cattails, green carpets of winter wheat, and giant cottonwoods along the river. There were old barns in good shape and buck-and-rail fences—rare, for that part of the country—and old rusting farm equipment, antique harrows and plows and stone boats resting on the sides of the gravelly hills. Wild rose and chokecherry cloaked the steep folds along the sides of the canyon. It would be a beautiful place to shoot a rooster.

"Do you think you can make it over to that canyon?" Robert asked.

Jack took a moment to answer. "Yes," he said and both men understood that Jack meant, *Yes, this year.*

They set off slowly. The dogs trotted along beside them, no longer hunting, the older dog conserving his energy for when they got back into the game and the younger dog impatient. The birds in the back of the men's game vests rested warmly against their backs. The frost was gone from the fields, though the fields glistened from where frost had been.

They reached the top of the canyon and looked down into it. The horses they'd seen the day before stood in the canyon. There were the large geldings and the one bluish roan. A few of the horses whisked their tails noncommittally.

"They look like they don't see people very often," Jack said.

"Not hunters, anyway," Robert said.

At the sound of their voices, the roosters hidden in the draws cackled and fell silent.

"What in the world do you suppose they're trying to tell us?" Jack asked.

Robert laughed. "Not to hunt them," he said.

They gestured the dogs down into the bottom and entered the brushy draw. Thorns pulled at their clothing, and the first few birds that got up flew directly into the sun, so that the men couldn't tell if they were hens or roosters. It was hard hunting, moving through all the brush, and they had no clear shots. The birds kept running ahead of them, racing down the hill and flushing just out of range of their guns.

The blue horse and his herd stood still, watching the men and dogs make their slow way down.

Near the bottom, Robert's little pointer finally set a bird. The men moved in, knowing by the perfection of the dog's point that they could take the bird. The only question was which man would take the shot, which would depend on whether the bird flew left or right. They reached the dog and waited for the bird to panic and leap into the sky.

Nothing happened. Robert kicked at the brush where his dog was pointing, trying to get the bird to flush.

"Could be a hen," Jack said. Sometimes the hens held tighter.

"Could be a big old smart rooster," Robert said. Sometimes the oldest and smartest ones held on until the hunters let down their guard and decided there was no bird, and then it would fly.

The dog blinked, whined, and cut his glowing green eyes up at Robert, asking permission to creep in closer, and Robert nodded. "Okay"

"Maybe it's hurt," Jack said. "Or may it's a dead bird that some other hunter shot and couldn't find."

The dog quivered with taut muscles and looked down over its quarry. Jack kicked at the brush, and the dog, unable to stand the tension, leapt forward and came up with a mouth full of porcupine quills.

The dog choked and gagged, retched, but then stepped forward and bit at the porcupine again, filling the last untouched reaches of its mouth and face with the ivory quills.

Robert shouted, "*No!*" and the rooster hiding just behind the porcupine blossomed into the sky and sailed away.

The dog kept after the porcupine, and Robert had to tackle the dog. Then Jack held the struggling animal in a headlock while Robert tried to pull out the quills, one by bloody one, with a pair of hemostats he carried for such incidents.

The dog was so strong that in its sideways writhing and wriggling, it carried Jack with it. Jack held on as if bulldogging a steer, and Robert chased the sliding mass of dog and man, and plucked quill after quill. There were easily a hundred in his mouth, and with each extracting, the dog howled ferociously, and a stream of blood issued from its mouth.

The dog snapped at the quills lodged in its tongue and the roof of its mouth, and the snapping only drove the quills deeper into the bony palate and the bleeding tongue.

It took three hours of wrestling before Robert had pulled all the quills he could reach. In that time their sliding struggles carried them all the way down the hill, through brush and thorn; they had cleared a wandering swath of almost a hundred yards in their wrestling, and the men and the dog were coated in sand and blood and dried leaves. They resembled the gravel-clad pupal stages of some monstrous aquatic insect.

After three hours of baying, the dog had no voice left, and little strength. All it could utter was an anguished hissing.

The men were even more exhausted than the dog. They turned him loose and lay there for a long time, too weary to get up.

The blue horse stood by, watching indifferently.

Jack and Robert decided to head back. They climbed out of the canyon, feeling that the birds had trounced them. Jack labored harder than ever, and they stopped and looked down one more time on the seeming idyll below.

The horse had not moved. It was watching them. It was a beautiful horse: blue on a green lawn.

"I feel like I just had my ass kicked," Jack said.

Robert smiled. "It's one we'll remember."

They had miles to go. They stuck out across the birdless stubble and after a long march reached the strange, abandoned railroad tracks laid across the prairie. The men turned south and followed the tracks, amazed at the pleasure of easier walking.

They came to the abandoned boxcars, in the lee of which was the only shade for miles. The dogs were panting, and the men sat down in the shade and rested and stared out to the horizon. They felt the inexplicable sweetness of looking to the horizon and seeing no beginning, no end, only raw country, hope, possibility.

"Reckon it's open?" Robert asked. They were seated at the steps of the old dining car.

"My legs hurt. You go see," Jack said.

There were three steps leading up to the dining car. Robert stood and went up and opened the door.

"Come on in," he said, and Jack slowly raised himself and went inside.

The interior was dusty. Days and nights of ceaseless prairie wind had pushed grit and sand through every seam and crevice. The car was warm, though, and it felt good to be in out of the wind.

Tablecloths were set at the dining tables. The men collapsed into the seats while the dogs trotted up and down the aisle, sniffing. A fly crawled sluggishly up one of the dusty windows.

The men spread their lunches on the old tablecloth. Dust rose from the table. They found old bottles of wine in the kitchen and opened several before finding one that hadn't turned. They filled their wineglasses and sipped, watching the afternoon light crawl slowly across the stubble outside, so that as they sat there, it seemed that the train might be traveling.

The dogs found a corner and piled up in it to nap. Robert cleaned one of the pheasants. There was still gas to fire the kitchen oven. Robert cut the bird into strips and salted and peppered it and cooked it in a skillet, searing it quickly in its own yellow fat. They wiped off the dusty formal dishes and silverware and ate the pheasant with wine, cheese, and apples from their lunches.

"Bread would be nice," Robert said. "I wish we'd brought some bread."

Outside the shadows of the stubble grew longer. Buttery light spread across the prairie. The light was flowing, it seemed to them, like the rising waters of some slow, calm tide—and they could feel the warmth in the boxcar fading, could hear the slightly irregular creaking of the heated metal as it began once more to contract as if obeying the pulse of some damaged but not quite broken metronome.

For a long time, Jack had the sensation that the creeping yellow light was coming in, rising higher, to take the power from his legs—to deliver to him, perhaps that afternoon, the curse of his father and grandfather, his uncles and brothers and great-uncles and male cousins—but after resting there a while longer, and after the second glass of wine, he began to feel better, as if the blood-tide of dense yellow light had reversed and was taking the pain and weakness away, back toward whatever distant place it had originated—back, once again, one more time, if only for a little while.

When they had finished their meal, and the second bottle of wine, they rose and cleaned their dishes, rinsing them with water from their canteens and drying them and resetting the table, and then they woke their dogs and went on out of the boxcar and into the crispness of advancing October.

They drove back to the compound to pay for the day's hunting, and to pick up their birds from the day before, and to say their good-byes.

There were more leaves on the ground than there had been the day before, and girls in their blue-and-white-checked dresses and black hats were raking the leaves into large piles of yellow and orange. There was no wind that afternoon, down in the river bottom, and some of the older boys were in charge of burning the piles of leaves before the wild evening winds came up and spread the leaves back over the yards; a few piles smoldered already, wisps of gray threads rising from beneath and within the dense bounty of leaves. An old woman sat on the steps of her house, carving a pumpkin, and when she looked up and smiled at Jack and Robert as they drove past, they were struck by how much her teeth looked like those on the jack-o'-lantern she was carving.

In the distance, they saw a group of men surrounding a yellow backhoe and working men with shovels, the men and machine laboring steadily in the yard, beneath the shade of a huge cottonwood. Mounds of fresh-turned earth were piled all around the men.

"Must have misplaced their strongbox," Jack said, "their gold doubloons," and Robert laughed.

From the other end of the compound, they saw Claire come running toward them, holding her skirt as she ran—running as if she had been waiting and watching for them. She waved at them as she ran, and when she drew up to their truck, she was breathless, and her bonnet had slipped back a bit, and they saw then what they had not seen the day before, that she was nearly as old as they were—in her late thirties, or maybe even into her early forties.

Over by the big cottonwood, the men paused one by one in their digging, until they were all watching, including Henry Bone. They stared for long moments—it seemed odd, unnatural, for all of them to have ceased in their movements—until finally one of them resumed his work, and then another, and another, until all of them except Bone were digging again. Some of the men climbed down into the hole, and finally Bone turned back to his work; and through it all, the yellow backhoe kept growling and reaching, groping with its mechanical claw, chuffing black smoke like charcoal etched into the blue sky.

The men went on toward Bone's home to settle up. Claire went with them, and as they walked, she reached behind them to take the birds from their game bags, then she looked at the men searchingly, wondering why there were only four birds and not six.

"That's it," Jack said. "One of the dogs got into a porcupine. We quit early."

At the word *porcupine,* Claire had whipped her head around to look at Bone, who was halfway back down into the hole; then she turned to Jack and Robert with an almost angry, disbelieving expression.

"Come with me," she said, and carrying the pheasants, she led them into the big community kitchen, where her sister, her mother, and her daughters were washing dishes.

That day the cooks had roasted an entire steer, boiled fifty potatoes and a hundred carrots, and baked a dozen loaves of bread. The old kitchen was dense with the aromas.

The husk of the steer lay upturned on an immense cutting board, the steer's ribs gleaming in yellow lamplight like the spars of a wrecked dory. There were a few fragments of pink flesh glistening on it, and Claire's sister went over the giant carcass with a shining meat cleaver and carved the last meat from the bones. She placed the scraps between slices of fresh bread, with no mayonnaise, mustard, lettuce, or cheese, only the juice of the meat to be used as dressing, and handed the sandwiches to Jack and Robert.

They thanked her and, sandwiches in hand, followed Claire to the dining room, where the sect took most of their meals together. The wood-plank floors were worn smooth, and, seeing the men admiring the gold grain of the wood, Claire said that the room had once served as a dance hall, before the sect had decided to outlaw dancing.

"Why'd you outlaw it?" Robert asked.

"There was some trouble between the sexes," Claire said. She made a dismissive gesture with her hand. "It was a long time ago. I'd like to see them give it another try."

The late daylight was soft on the old floors and on the dark cherrywood of the tables and benches.

"Do you remember it?" Robert asked.

Claire nodded. "I was fifteen," she said. "It was good. I thought it would always be that way."

Outside, in the wind, leaves were falling past the windows. Leaves were landing on the tin roof and sliding down, and Claire shifted and looked out the window. She seemed to Robert to move with a memory of dance.

She still had the pheasants in her arms. She turned again and led Jack and Robert out of the dining room, into the main yard outside, and toward the house. There, she insisted on cleaning the new birds. The men sat at the table, and she hummed and sang a German song as she worked.

Jack shifted in his chair and massaged his thighs. Robert had never seen him admit pain in front of a stranger. Jack had told him that Cecelia massaged his legs when they were hurting, and Robert had thought, *Just you wait, enjoy it now, because it's not going to last.*

Robert let out a small gasp and sought to push the terror back, the lovelessness. Claire continued her song. It was a psalm or a hymn, utterly beautiful and peaceful.

"What does it mean?" Robert asked. "What are you singing?"

"It's the 'Morning Song,' " Claire said. She had finished the birds. She looked euphoric, aglow. She said, "The sun rises. It *is* glorious. For this I give thanks, O Lord. The sun is glorious. Your will is glorious. Humble me and teach me to do your will. Your will is the morning sunlight, your will is glorious, your work is glorious, teach me to love you. Don't let a moment lie idle, alleluia. Teach me, teach me glory. Thank you for the loving morning, so we may work. Amen."

Jack glanced at his watch. "You sing it all day?"

Claire smiled. "It was my aunt's song. She made it up. She used to sing it first thing every morning. I like to sing it all day. She died two weeks ago. She was a beautiful singer. I sing it now. It reminds me of her. She was too young," Claire said. "She was only fifty-six."

"What did she die of?" Jack asked.

Claire shrugged, drying her hands on a dish towel. "I don't know," she said. "She got real small and tired, and then she died."

"The words are so much prettier in their own language," Robert said. "The sound of them, I mean." Claire nodded and repeated the words in German, speaking them slowly.

"We teach it to the children in school," she said proudly. "It helps them learn the language. Ours is a dialect, and a mix of languages, unknown anywhere else in the world."

The pheasants had finished draining in the sink, and she wrapped them in freezer paper and labeled them with the date. She put them in a sack. Her eyes were shining, and Robert thought she was seeing through and beyond her visitors, seeing God in them, and that was why she smiled.

"Do you two want to see my worms?" she asked. "I sell them to fishermen. Do you know any fishermen who need to buy worms? Come on, I'll show you."

With her long skirt gathered in one hand, she led them out to a toolshed. She took a flashlight down from a shelf, lifted the lid of a wooden box, and shone the light down onto damp, black soil mixed with coffee grounds. There were thousands of worms in the box.

"I dug them all summer, kept them fed and watered, but nobody wanted any," Claire said. "I dug too many."

She shone her light on the back of her shed, where jars of jam and syrup were stacked several feet deep and high to the ceiling, a lifetime's supply of jam and syrup, two lifetimes' worth. Robert felt dizzy and stepped back out into the sunlight. He leaned against a tree, and Claire came out and looked at him curiously.

They walked back toward the house, Jack limping badly, and Claire moved in beside him and put his arm around her shoulders, so he could lean on her. Back in her kitchen, they added up what was owed for the day's hunting, some jam and syrup purchased, and for the birds cleaned. Then Bone came in, begrimed from working on a break in a buried water pipe, and Claire rose from her chair like some startled bird.

"We didn't do anything," she said.

She was talking about the money—no money had changed hands yet.

Bone leaned over the table and studied the accounting ciphered in pencil on the back of an envelope. He made a short grunt, seemingly a *yes*, and counted out money onto the table.

Looking at the money, Robert felt outside himself. He saw Claire's hand swoop in and separate a share of the money, now fives and ones, and put it in her apron pocket. She looked at Bone and gave a satisfied smile.

Robert felt sorry for her and reached across the table and patted her hand. He covered hers with his for a moment.

She looked up quickly but didn't flinch. She took her hand from his and brushed her eyes.

Bone said, "Here, what's all this about?" He pointed at Robert's hand.

"What's that shit all over your hand? Those punctures. Looks like you got snakebit. What's all that?"

"We got them fooling with a porcupine," Jack blurted. He held out his hands to show the same marks.

"What do you mean," Bone said, "*fooling* with the porcupine?"

Jack shrugged. "One of the dogs got into one. It took us darn near three hours to pull all the quills."

"Did you shoot the porcupine?" Bone said. "Where was it? Did you kill it?"

"Down the draw north of here," Jack said. "Down in the chokecherries. No, we didn't kill it."

"You just cost me two hundred dollars," Bone said. "Why, when one of my cows gets quills stuck in her nose from sniffing the damn thing, it will be you boys' *fault*." And the look on Bone's face said, *You stupid fool.*

Claire tilted her chin down, a gesture to restrain her husband, who turned and stared out the window. Claire lightly cleared her throat, and the men understood they were released.

The men shook Claire's hand and then Bone's and went out to their truck. Jack's legs felt as if they had been beaten with a baseball bat, and he wobbled as he walked.

ROBERT COULD NOT WAIT to get home. They drove up out of the river bottom and out across the almost endless stubble.

"I didn't like that old sonofabitch," Robert said, "but I'll have to hand it to him, I don't know how in hell one man can take care of twenty-six thousand acres. That's sick," he said. "That's twisted. *Jesus*," he said, "which would you rather do: manage a colony of religious fanatics and twenty-six thousand acres, or saunter the fields at your leisure with a gun and a dog in the early autumn?"

Jack laughed, "I can't believe you took that lady's hand."

They drove on silently admiring the blue shadows sliding in over the countryside.

"I don't guess we'll be invited to hunt there again," Jack said.

"He'll have us back," Robert said. "As long as we're willing to pay, he'll have us back."

"I'm not so sure," Jack said.

They entered the town of Mammon. On Main Street shocks of hay were piled against the parking meters in decoration for Halloween and Thanksgiving. Bright pumpkins were stacked beneath storefront windows. Ears of dried corn hung from the doors of businesses, and as the daylight faded against the old red stone buildings, Robert felt despair stirring in him again. In the street ahead a young woman crossed with two small boys, holding their hands.

Christ, Robert thought. *Christ, I can't give up.* Now that the hunt was over, there was only himself and Jennifer to think of.

"Would you mind," he asked, "if I went back and got that blue horse?"

Jack's truck was parked at the hotel, just a few blocks ahead. He was already looking forward to the drive home. Robert would head west, and Jack south. If Jack hurried, he might get home before Cecelia went to sleep.

"What do you mean?" Jack asked cautiously.

"I mean to buy it from them. Go back there and get it. I'll take it home to Jennifer for a surprise, a present."

"How do you know it's for sale?" Jack asked.

"It'll be for sale," Robert said. "It's just a horse, to them."

Jack hesitated. "How would you get it home?"

"I'll buy a trailer," Robert said, pulling into the parking lot of the feed store. It was five minutes to six: right at closing time.

"Can you afford it?" Jack asked. The impulse added up easily to at least a couple thousand dollars, and Jack knew how poor Robert was. His life was hand-to-mouth.

"I'll figure it out," Robert said. "I've got to. How often do you see a blue horse?"

"Never," Jack agreed, still alarmed.

"Jennifer will love it," Robert said.

"Oh, I don't know," Jack said. A pause, as he tried to plumb the depths of such hope, even desperation. "I don't know," he said again, cautiously. "What if you buy it and drive it all the way out there and she doesn't . . ." Jack paused again, unsure of what he wanted to say. "What if she doesn't see it quite the same way you do? Then what?"

"She'll love it," Robert said.

Behind the store was a horse trailer being used to store hay. Robert bought the trailer and some hay for a thousand dollars. He hooked the trailer to his truck and turned around and drove back out toward the compound in the dusk.

"You don't know they'll sell you that horse," Jack said. "You might have bought a horse trailer for nothing."

"They'll sell," Robert said.

The trailer rattled and clattered behind them as they went down the road to the compound. Sparks bounced from beneath the trailer when it scraped against chert, and in the compound window squares of faces peered out at the din.

"Poor tired fuckers are already ready for bed," Robert said.

They pulled around to the side of Bone's house and saw he was still out in a ditch, working on the broken water pipe. Claire came out and stood in the yard to watch.

Jack stayed in the truck. Robert went over to Bone and explained what he wanted. He offered six hundred dollars.

Bone laughed and kept working. He didn't come out of the ditch until Robert was up over a thousand dollars.

Bone lit a cigarette and smoked, and when Robert's offer didn't go past twelve hundred, he surmised that was all the cash Robert had.

Claire watched, thinking what a difference twelve hundred dollars would mean in the coming year.

Bone wanted one of Robert's guns, not for himself, Robert thought, but to sell. Robert wouldn't give up the gun, and in the end they settled on twelve hundred and Robert giving back the pheasants he'd shot and all the honey and jam and syrup he'd bought too.

"Carry the jams and such over to her," Bone said, pointing to Claire after he pocketed the money. "And the birds. We'll eat 'em tomorrow."

Robert took it all to Claire, who held out her apron like a basket to receive it all. She leaned slightly forward as she received the bounty.

Robert looked at her, then turned quickly away and walked back to his truck. Bone was standing there talking idle farmer talk with Jack.

The three men rode out to the field, Bone in his own truck, and Jack and Robert in theirs. A rising quarter moon sliced its crescent through the bare branches of the cotton-woods. The men parked. The horses were silhouettes in the field. They would come to the men, grazing their way toward them out of curiosity.

"We might get off easy," Bone said. "Ain't none of 'em ever been in a trailer before, so they might not even know enough to be scared of it." Robert could smell the fresh earth on Bone, and he wondered if Bone would bathe in the river before going to bed or if he would simply crawl into his bed begrimed.

"Put some of that hay out for them," Bone advised, and they took armfuls of sweet dry hay and moved among the herd, giving them flakes of the hay. Robert marveled at being in the midst of the animals' breath, the warmth of their bod-ies, the sound of their teeth grinding the hay, their hooves shuffling on the earth.

Bone slipped a hackamore over the blue horse's muzzle. "This wasn't part of the deal," he said, meaning the hackamore.

"You can send me twenty dollars when you get home." He tied the horse at the open tailgate of the trailer.

Then, taking a cigarette lighter from his pocket, he lit a handful of hay, and in the sudden blossoming of light, the other horses shied away, nickering their worry. The blue horse pulled back, rising straight up on its hind legs as the lead rope went taut. The horse pawed the air and whinnied wildly.

It didn't have to be this way, Robert thought, holding the trailer door. *We could have taken our time.*

Bone moved quickly now, waving the burning hay at the horse in slashes of light, while the blue horse lunged and twisted, trying to get free. The hay burned out, singeing Bone's hands. He cursed and picked up more hay and lit it. The horse reared, jerking the trailer, then lunged forward, banging against the trailer but refusing to go into it.

Bone rushed and feinted at the horse, waving the burning hay in its face and then slashing at its withers with the heated straw, and suddenly, with a scream of rage, the horse was up into the trailer, and Jack and Robert quickly slammed the doors shut and bolted the hasp.

Bone tossed the burning hay down to the ground, and it died out. The horse thumped around inside the trailer.

"It's late," Bone said. "I got to get home." He got in his truck and drove away with his headlights off. The horse inside the trailer was screaming.

"It'll calm down," Robert said. "We'll get down the road a ways, and it'll get tired of kicking. It'll settle down." He was alarmed by the horse's fury but exhilarated too. He felt sure that he had done the right thing.

He took Jack back to Mammon, and all the way there the horse continued screaming and kicking. In town, the racket seemed louder.

At Jack's truck they said their farewells. "Good luck," Jack said, nodding at the trailer. The horse had stopped screaming but was still kicking and thrashing. They shook hands, and each man headed home.

THE TRAILER kept rattling and shaking, buffeting behind him, and from time to time, Robert pulled over and went around back to try to console the furious horse, but the animal would have nothing to do with him.

It'll calm down yet, Robert thought. They still had a long way to go.

The horse battled on, kicking and screaming through the night, troubling the sleep of the residents of Great Falls, Choteau, Dupuyer, Browning, Kalispell, Libby, then into Idaho, Bonners Ferry and Sandpoint. Into Washington, then, Newport, and up into Okanogan and Methow.

Robert arrived home in the early dawn. The children were asleep. Jennifer was sitting out on the porch in a heavy robe and blanket, drinking a cup of steaming coffee. Twenty years, they'd been married. It didn't seem like a long time.

It's going to be the most beautiful thing she's ever seen, he told himself. *From here on, everything's going to change. This is it,* he told himself, *we finally made it, we finally crossed some hard threshold. We made it.*

There was a small moment of deep panic as he shut off the engine. As if he had already lived this moment—as if the moment existed on the other side of a pane of glass, and he could see across to where he was going. It seemed for an instant that both he and she had already been in this place and time a hundred times before, and when he stepped forward and she asked, "What is in the trailer?" and he told her about the blue horse, showed her the blue horse, she had merely looked at him and said, "We can't have a horse." It seemed to him, in the already-living, that her face had colored. That she had said, "We don't have time or room for it. They eat too much. They're too hard to take care of in winter. They need too much water. We don't *need* a horse. What do you mean, a *blue* horse?"

"You've got to take it back," she would say. "I don't want a horse." "Take it back to wherever it came from. What were you thinking?"

And rather than disappointment, Robert might feel a strange sense of relief—a kind of freedom. "You're right," he would say. "I don't know what I was thinking. Maybe I was thinking things could change. Maybe I was thinking things could go back to how they were. But you're right," he would say. "It was a mistake."

"They don't make a horse like that," she would say, in his recollection of the thing-not-yet-happened, "the one you're thinking of. Take it back."

Robert sat in his truck, thinking, *Why didn't I listen to Jack?* Thinking, *There's no way this is going to work.* Amazed by the depth and breadth of his hope.

Courage, he told himself and got out of the truck, bleary-eyed from the drive, and walked up the porch steps and kissed her.

"What's in the trailer?" she asked. The horse had stopped screaming and wasn't kicking anymore but was simply chuffing and panting, as if resting up for another round. Robert imagined that he could feel the horse's heat and anger emanating from the trailer.

"A horse," Robert said. "A blue horse. It's for you. It's a present."

Jennifer stared at him disbelievingly. Robert closed his eyes. *It's blue*, he thought, with every fiber of his being. *It's blue*.

When he opened his eyes she was watching him, and the trailer, cautiously: not as if he or it were the enemy, but with something, he thought—he wanted to believe—that might be almost like hope, and curiosity. For once he didn't know what she was going to say next, but he was listening.